W9-DFD-326

Emerald
meeow
CAT
FOOD

by Jane Thayer

Pictures by Seymour Fleishman

William Morrow & Company
New York

Printed in the United States of America.

Library of Congress Catalog Card Number 70-85408

Emerald was a cat
who didn't know he was a cat.
He thought he was people.

He lived in a house
(with Mrs. Bucklestone),
like people.
He slept on a bed, like people.
He ate out of dishes, like people.
He even sat on a chair
and watched television like people.
It never entered Emerald's head
that he wasn't people.

Emerald sat on his front steps
enjoying the air.
He saw strange cats going by.
He said, "Strange cats going by."
But he never said hello to cats.
Because he wasn't a cat.

One night Emerald
had been out for a stroll
before he went to bed.
He was sitting in front of the door,
waiting for it to open,
when a strange cat came by.
The strange cat said,
"Ha! *You* are the cat
who doesn't know he's a cat."

"I am not a cat," said Emerald indignantly.
The strange cat said,
"You are too. I can prove it."
Emerald said, "You can not."
Then he said, "How can you?"
The strange cat said, "Come with me."
Emerald knew he was people,
but he wondered how the strange cat
could prove he was a cat.
The door didn't open so he went along.

The strange cat said,
"Look at that moon. Isn't it beautiful?"
Emerald said, "Yes!"
The strange cat said,
"Well, that proves you're a cat.
Cats always think the moon is beautiful.
Come on."

They came to a fence.
Some cats were sitting on the fence
practicing their songs in the moonlight.
Emerald jumped on the fence
and began to practice his songs too.

The strange cat said,
"That proves you're a cat.
Cats always practice their songs
on the fence in the moonlight."
Emerald thought,
I did enjoy practicing my songs.
But I'm not a cat.
The strange cat said, "Come on."

They went through a garden.
The strange cat said,
"Do you smell something delicious?"
Emerald sniffed and said, "Mm!"
The strange cat said,
"That is catnip growing.
Cats always think catnip smells delicious.
Have a taste."
Emerald nibbled.
The strange cat said, "Is it good?"

Emerald rolled over and over,
it was so good!
The strange cat said,
"Well, you're certainly a cat.
Nobody likes catnip but cats."
Emerald said, "They don't?"
He said doubtfully,
"I *thought* I was *people*."
The strange cat said, "Come on."

They went through a field.
Emerald heard a rustling in the grass.
Suddenly away he went,
chasing the rustle in the grass.

The strange cat said, “That was a mouse.
Do you like to chase mice in the grass?”
Emerald said, “Oh, yes!”
“No question about your being a cat,”
said the strange cat.
“Come on.”

They went into the dark woods
where the moon shone through the trees.
They had mysterious adventures.

The strange cat said,
"Do you like mysterious adventures?"
Emerald said, "Yes, they're fun!"
The strange cat said,
"That proves without a doubt
that you're a cat.
Cats always like mysterious adventures."
Emerald said, "They do?"
He said, "I guess I'm a cat.
And all the time I thought I was people!"
The strange cat smiled.

“Since I’m a cat,” cried Emerald,
“I am going to live outdoors from now on!
I am going to sit on the fence
and practice my songs
in the moonlight.
I am going
to catch mice.

I am going to eat
delicious fresh catnip every day.
I am going to have
some more of these mysterious adventures.
I am never," cried Emerald,
"going home to watch television!"

Just then, far away,
Mrs. Bucklestone called
in a clear high voice,
"Here, Emerald, Emerald, Emerald!"
Emerald practically always went home
when Mrs. Bucklestone called,
because usually it was mealtime.
"Excuse me,"
he said to the strange cat.
"Good-by, I have to go."
And off he leaped.
He forgot about living outdoors.

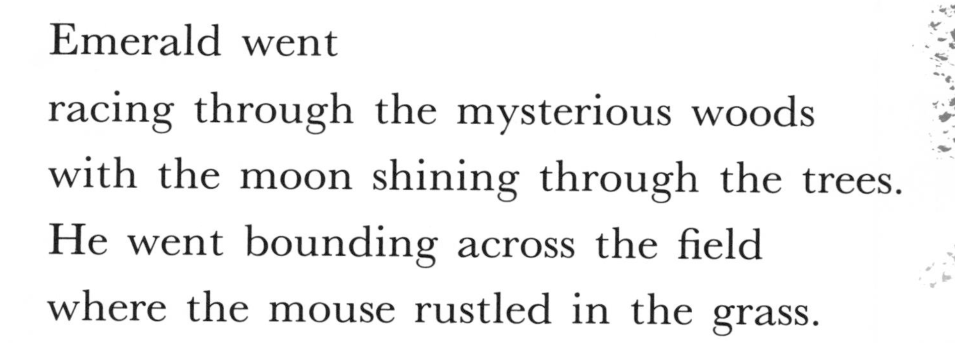

Emerald went
racing through the mysterious woods
with the moon shining through the trees.
He went bounding across the field
where the mouse rustled in the grass.

He streaked past the catnip
growing in the garden.
He jumped the fence
where the cats were practicing songs.

He shot straight through
the open front door
that Mrs. Bucklestone closed behind him.
"Where have you been?"
said Mrs. Bucklestone,
and gave him a dish of milk.

When Emerald finished the milk
he took a bath.
He went in and sat on his chair
and watched television.
But he kept thinking about the moonlight,
and the cats practicing their songs,
and catnip.
He thought, Possibly I *could* be a cat.
He thought about the mouse in the grass
and mysterious adventures in the woods.
He thought, Could I *possibly* be a cat?

When the two clocks in the house
had both struck ten o'clock,
Mrs. Bucklestone turned off the television.
She locked the door.
She carried Emerald upstairs
and put him on a warm blanket
on the foot of her bed.
She went to bed.

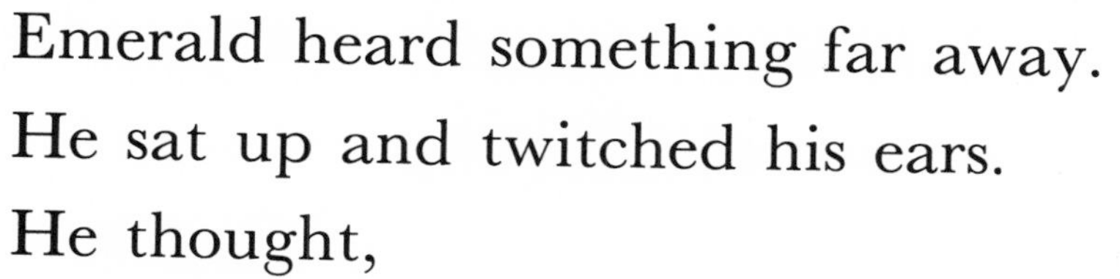

Emerald heard something far away.
He sat up and twitched his ears.
He thought,
I wish I were out in the moonlight
having mysterious adventures.

Then he heard nothing more,
and finally he snuggled down
on the blanket.
The blanket felt so soft and warm
that suddenly Emerald didn't want
to be anywhere else in the world.
He thought sleepily,
Silly, wasn't I!
Thinking I was a cat!

Emerald
HOME
SWEET
HOME
1084